The Story Of
RUMPELSTILTSKIN

First published in Great Britain by HarperCollins Publishers Ltd in 1991
First published in this edition in Picture Lions in 1996
3 5 7 9 10 8 6 4
Picture Lions is an imprint of the Children's Division, part of HarperCollins
Publishers Ltd, 77-85 Fulham Palace Road, Hammersmith, London W6 8JB.
Text and illustrations copyright © Jonathan Langley 1991
The author/illustrator asserts the moral right to
be identified as the author/illustrator of the work.
ISBN: 0 00 664070 2
Printed in Italy by L.E.G.O.

THE STORY OF
RUMPELSTILTSKIN

RETOLD & ILLUSTRATED BY
JONATHAN LANGLEY

PictureLions
An Imprint of HarperCollinsPublishers

Once upon a time, long, long ago, when mountains were
more pointed and there was a king in every castle, there
lived a miller who was forever telling tall stories. The
miller had a daughter called Ruby, who was very clever, and
he was always boasting about the things she could do.

Once he boasted that his daughter sang so beautifully that the birds came out at night and flew around the moon. Another time he said his daughter could juggle four hedgehogs with one hand and make a dozen fruit cakes with the other.

These stories were so silly that his neighbours just laughed when they heard them, but one day the King was in town and he heard one of the miller's stories.

"My daughter is so clever that she can spin straw into gold," the miller said.

The King loved gold and, when he heard the miller's boast, he ordered Ruby to be brought to his castle and led her to a small room where there was a spinning wheel and straw piled up to the ceiling.

"Spin this straw into gold by morning or you will be fed to the Royal Crocodiles," the King said, and locked her in.

Poor Ruby was both cross and frightened. "What has my stupid father done now. I can't spin straw into gold," she said. She looked at the straw and thought about the Royal Crocodiles and began to cry.

Suddenly a funny little man appeared and skipped around
the room. "Well now, what's all this? Why are you
crying?" he said.

"I must spin this straw into gold and I don't know
how," answered Ruby.

The little man smiled and said, "What will you give me
if I spin the straw into gold for you?"

"I will give you my necklace," said Ruby.

"Very well," said the little man and held out his hand. Ruby gave him the necklace and he put it in his pocket. Then he sat down at the spinning wheel and started to spin. He really was spinning straw into gold!

All through the night the little man worked at the spinning wheel and, by morning, all the straw was gone and in its place was a heap of glistening gold thread. Ruby stared at the gold in amazement.

"Oh thank you," she said to the little man, but he'd disappeared.

When the King came and unlocked the door he gasped at the sight of all the gold. He thought Ruby was indeed very clever, but he was a very greedy King. That night he took Ruby to a bigger room with a spinning wheel and straw piled up to the ceiling.

"Spin this straw into gold by morning or you will be fed to the Royal Crocodiles," the King said, and again he locked her in.

Ruby sat at the spinning wheel and tried to spin the straw but all she made was dust. "Oh, if only that little man could help me," she cried.

"Here I am," said a voice, and there he was again. "What will you give me if I spin all this straw into gold for you?" said the funny little man.

"I will give you my ring," said Ruby, and quickly put it in his hand.

He smiled and sat down at the spinning wheel. Again the little man worked busily all night and in the morning, when all the straw was gone and in its place was a bigger heap of glistening gold, he disappeared.

At sunrise the King came and unlocked the door. He was delighted to see all the gold. "You are indeed very, very, clever," he said, but he was a very, very, greedy king and he wanted even more.

That night he took Ruby to an even bigger room with a spinning wheel and straw piled up to the ceiling.

"Spin this straw into gold by morning or you will be fed to the Royal Crocodiles," the King said, and once again he locked her in.

Ruby looked at the mountain of straw and said, "Oh, what am I to do? Only that little man can help me now."

"Here I am," said a voice, and once again there he was. "What will you give me if I spin all this straw into gold for you?" said the funny little man.

"I have nothing more to give you," said Ruby.

"Then promise to give me your first baby when you are Queen," said the little man.

Ruby thought this could never happen, so she promised.

Once again the little man worked all night at the spinning wheel until all the straw was gone and in its place was a huge heap of glistening gold. Then, as before, he disappeared.

Once more the King came and unlocked the door. He was overjoyed to see all the gold. "You are the cleverest in all my kingdom," he said. "Marry me and we will be rich for ever."

Ruby was a bit shocked but, since there was no more talk of crocodiles, she said, "Yes."

Soon there was a grand Royal Wedding and Ruby and the King were married. They were very happy together and, when their first baby was born, they were even happier, but Queen Ruby forgot her promise to the little man.

One day he came when Queen Ruby was alone and reminded her. She cried and cried until, at last, the little man said, "If you can guess my name in three days you can keep your child." Then he disappeared.

All day and night Ruby sat thinking of all the names she knew, and she sent messengers all over the kingdom to find new ones.

Next day, when the little man came, Queen Ruby said, "Is it Thomas, Kevin, or Michael?"

"No, no, no," said the little man, and skipped away.

The next day Queen Ruby tried more unusual names. "Is it Bandylegs, Jellybottom, or Crookshanks?"

"No, no, no," said the little man skipping away. "If you can't guess my name tomorrow, I will take the baby."

On the morning of the third day Queen Ruby was feeling very unhappy when a messenger returned and said, "Yesterday I was in the great dark wood, when I came upon a funny little house. In front of the house was a fire, and a strange little man was dancing around the fire singing:

> 'Hocus pocus, dance and sing
> First a necklace, then a ring
> Riddles and magic are my game
> RUMPELSTILTSKIN is my name!'"

Queen Ruby jumped for joy. "Thank you, thank you!" she said to the messenger and gave her a bag of gold.

When the funny little man appeared, Queen Ruby
pretended not to know and said, "Is your name Jack, or is
it Percy, or is it ...

RUMPELSTILTSKIN?"

"Aaaaahh!! Someone told you!" shouted the little man. He jumped about, all in a rage, and stamped his foot so hard it went through the floor where it stuck fast. Red in the face, he pulled and pulled at his leg, then, with a cry of anger, he disappeared in a puff of smoke.

Ruby lived happily ever after. She was a good Queen and well loved by the people and, after the birth of her second child, it was decreed that she and her children should rule the country, leaving the King to count his treasure.

The King had a long life but one day, whilst he was carrying a heavy sack of gold, he accidentally fell into the Royal Crocodile Pool and was never seen again.